The Author

"Hello, friends! It's Whiffy here.
Whiffy McPumpernickel! From soaring skies to
mysterious forests, I've adventured far and wide,
meeting the most fascinating characters. So,
snuggle up and get ready for a heart-warming
tale about my frosty friend, Nigel."

www.whiffy.info

On an island where dragons roared and played,
and magical memories would never fade.

Lived young Nigel, with scales so bright,
But unlike others, he couldn't ignite."

Day in, day out, with persistence, he'd try,
Yearning for flames to light up the sky.

He'd give it his all, but it was really tough,
When nothing happened, not even a puff.

Day after day, Nigel gave it his best.
He didn't want to be different, just like the rest.

He'd huff, and he'd puff, but just had no spark
Was he destined to live his life in the dark?

The dragons would tease, they'd laugh and mock,
"Where's your flame, Nigel? Can you even talk?
For a dragon without fire, what use can you be?
You're as odd as a fish that can't swim in the sea!"

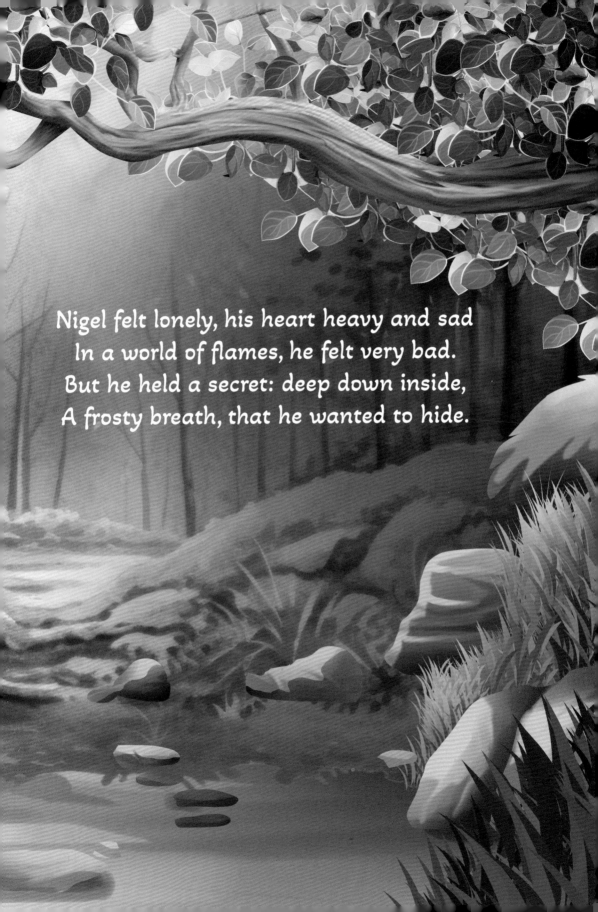

Nigel felt lonely, his heart heavy and sad
In a world of flames, he felt very bad.
But he held a secret: deep down inside,
A frosty breath, that he wanted to hide.

Every dragon showed off, spewing flames so high,
Nigel would watch with a tear in his eye.
While others boasted of their fiery display,
He'd hide in the shadows, keeping his frost at bay.

His breath was like snowflakes, gentle and cool,
In a world of blazing heat, he felt like a fool.
"Why am I not like them?" he'd silently cry,
Yearning for flames, gazing up at the sky.

But no dragon could tell, a danger was near,
A new time of reckoning, a time of fear,
Nigel's fortune was about to change,
His position in life would soon rearrange.

One fateful day, when the sun was so strong,
A spark ignited, and things went so wrong.
The island was in danger, the trees were alight,
All the dragons were hopeless and took to flight.

Their fiery breath could do nothing to help,
And the dragons' island started to melt.
But Nigel stepped forward, took a deep breath in,
And blew out frost; his face was a grin.

His icy breath spread, quenching the blaze,
Turning the fire to a cool blue haze.
The dragons watched on in utter surprise,
As the fire went out, right before their eyes.

But the fire was stubborn; in places it clung,
Nigel's work was far from done.

Another huge breath and a large puff of snow
He finally put out the last ember's glow

The island was safe, thanks to Nigel's might,
His frosty breath had set everything right.
The dragons who teased, now cheered,
and waved,
"Nigel's our hero, every dragon is saved".

"Your gift," they said, "is unique and rare,
And we were wrong to mock, to jeer and to glare.
For every dragon, be it fire or frost,
Has a special power, that should never be lost."

From that day on, Nigel soared high and free,
A hero, a friend, as proud as could be.
For he learned that day, and so did the rest,
That being different can truly be best.

Well, friends! It's Whiffy here. I hope you enjoyed the story about our friend Nigel.

If you'd like to read some more stories about some of my other magical friends, please let me know.

www.whiffy.info

The Below Colouring Book is Available

Nigel The Dragon's Colouring Book

50 Colouring Images
including characters from the book
"The Dragon Who Couldn't Breathe Fire"
by Whiffy McPumpernickle

First published in the UK in 2023 by
Independent Publishing Network.
Author: Whiffy McPumpernickle
www.whiffy.info
Please direct all enquiries to the author
ISBN: 9781805171126

Dedication

This book is dedicated to some magical friends who have helped me through my life's adventure. A huge thank-you to;
Wif, Moo, Ellie-Bellie-Boo, Bobster, and our beloved friends now gone, Mrs Rediculund & The Bunty.

See you in my next adventure

Love Whiffy xxx

Copyright © 2023 by the author and creator behind Whiffy McPumpernickle. All rights reserved. No part of this book may be reproduced in any form or by any electronic or mechanical means, including information storage and retrieval systems, without permission in writing from the author, except by reviewers, who may quote brief passages in a review.